WRONG EXIT

'We should be able to see the roundabout,' said Adam.

'There isn't one,' said Dave.

The wide road stretched ahead, absolutely straight, for a mile or more. The roundabout had disappeared, and so had the road that should have led us back to the car.

Where was it? Where was Mum? And where on earth were we?

SHARP SHADES

WRONG EXIT

Look out for other exciting stories
in the *Sharp Shades* series:

A Murder of Crows by Penny Bates
Shouting at the Stars by David Belbin
Witness by Anne Cassidy
Doing the Double by Alan Durant
Watch Over Her by Dennis Hamley
Tears of a Friend by Joanna Kenrick
Blitz by David Orme
Plague by David Orme
Sea Fever by Gillian Philip
Soldier Boy by Anne Rooney
Hunter's Moon by John Townsend

SHARP SHADES

WRONG EXIT

By Mary Chapman

Published by Evans Brothers Limited
2A Portman Mansions
Chiltern St
London W1U 6NR

British Library Cataloguing in Publication Data
Chapman, Mary
Wrong exit. - (Sharp shades)
1. Dystopias 2. Young adult fiction
I. Title
823.9'2[J]

ISBN-13: 9780237537296

Series Editor: David Belbin
Editor: Julia Moffatt
Designer: Rob Walster
Picture research: Bryony Jones

Picture acknowledgements:
istockphoto.com: pp 8, 16, 21, 30, 34, 44, 53, 58

Contents

Chapter One

December. Somewhere in Norfolk.

The fog closed in.

The fuel warning-light flashed.

Mum peered through the windscreen.

'We need petrol,' said Adam.

'There's a petrol station soon, just after we take the first exit at the next roundabout,' said Mum.

But the engine slowed down. The car jerked. Stopped.

'If it wasn't foggy we could see the roundabout and the petrol-station from here,' said Mum. 'There's an empty can in the boot. I'll go. You wait here. I won't be long.'

She disappeared into the fog. I looked at my watch: 5.54.

It was only a few miles to the cottage we were renting for Christmas. A funny time to go to the seaside but Mum wanted to do something different, our first Christmas since Dad left.

Fifteen minutes went by. No other cars passed.

'Mum's a long time,' said Ruby.

'It's probably further than she thought,' I said.

'I hope she brings some sweets,' said Ruby.

'I'll ring her,' said Adam.

He switched on his mobile; swore under his breath.

'No signal,' he said. 'Typical!'

'I'm hungry,' said Ruby, 'and my

feet are cold.'

'Let's have some biscuits. Then go and meet Mum,' I said. 'The walk'll warm us up.'

'I don't want to go out in the fog.'

'You'll get your sweets sooner. Here, have my watch and be timekeeper.'

'All right.'

We gobbled some biscuits and I stuffed the rest into my pocket. We grabbed our torches. I turned off the sidelights and locked the car.

'Twelve minutes past six,' said Ruby.

After a few yards I looked back;

the fog had devoured our car. I could see nothing behind, and nothing in front. I didn't like this at all.

Chapter Two

At the roundabout I asked Ruby the time.

'Exactly twenty-past six.'

We took the first exit, and the fog lifted, suddenly, completely. Now we could see by the light of our torches and the moon. But the road wasn't winding and narrow, like I remembered; it was wide, without trees or hedges. Had we taken the wrong exit?

'There's the petrol station,' said Adam.

But it wasn't lit up. As we got nearer, we saw the roof was caved in, windows smashed, tall grass growing around the pumps. Cars were parked higgledy-piggledy on the forecourt. I felt we shouldn't go any closer.

'Time check, Ruby!' I said as cheerfully as I could.

'Don't want to be time-keeper. It's boring.'

'Just have a quick peek.'

'Twenty-seven minutes past. Where's Mum? Do you think she's lost?'

'No. This is the only road until we reach the village. There aren't any turnings off. She must have kept going. She's probably at the cottage already.'

I tried to sound confident but I wasn't.

At last – the village sign: LITTLE THORNTON.

It leaned over, battered and muddy, green and brown stringy stuff clinging to it.

We turned up the lane to the cottage.

'Try your mobile again, Adam,' I said.

But there was still no signal. I hated feeling cut off from the rest of the world.

And there was this awful stench. I'd thought it was just a country smell at first, but it had got stronger. I knew what it was – drains, the smell of sewage.

Our cottage was at the top of the

hill. I imagined the door opening, light and warmth flooding out.

But there were no lights. Where was Mum? I had a horrible feeling in my stomach. I suppose it was terror.

'What time is it, Ruby?' I pushed her sleeve back. 'Quarter to seven. Let's go round the back. Mr Mason usually leaves the door unlocked ready for us.'

'Eeurgh!' said Ruby. 'What's that stinky smell? I'm going to be sick!'

'It's only the drains.'

'It's poo!' said Ruby.

We slithered and skidded along the path, past piles of broken paving stones and roof tiles. At the back of the house a faint light flickered in an upstairs window.

Adam pushed the door open.

Wet, slimy floor, covered in soggy paper, smashed bottles, sodden cardboard boxes. Worst of all – greyish-brownish things. Mice? Rats? The smell was horrendous.

We crept into the hall. A creaking sound. Floorboards? Someone above us? Squatters? Illegal immigrants? Drug-dealers? With knives? Guns?

Adam shone his torch on to the stairway – broken banisters, missing steps. Safer to stay down here.

'Anybody there?' I called.

Footsteps.

I shone my torch on to the landing, so we could see *them* before they saw us.

Chapter Three

'How many of you are there?' I shouted.

He wore dark clothes, a fleece, jeans tucked into wellingtons. Odd, wearing wellingtons upstairs. Must be a tramp.

I kept the torchlight on his face. He came down slowly.

'What are you doing in our cottage?' I demanded.

He wasn't very tall, about Adam's age; straggly, greasy hair, pale face streaked with dirt.

'It's not *your* cottage!'

'We've rented it for Christmas,' I said. 'Why are you here?'

'Only dry place I could find,' he said. 'I couldn't camp out in one of the caravans.'

'There aren't any caravans in Little Thornton.'

'Greenfield Caravan Site,' he said. 'My mum and dad's site.'

But there wasn't a caravan site in the village.

'Why's this the only dry place?' I asked.

'Because of the floods, last month.'

I remembered Mum telling us she'd heard there might be floods on the east coast, but they didn't happen.

'There weren't any,' I said.

'There were! The whole village was flooded. Everyone drowned. I'm the only one left. I managed to get up here and climb on to the roof. I stayed until the water went down.

Then I got in through a bedroom window. I've been here ever since.'

'But, Mum phoned Mr Mason last week,' said Adam. 'He didn't say anything about floods.'

'There's no Mr Mason here,' said the boy. 'And where's your mum anyway?'

'She went to get petrol – we'd run out. She didn't come back,' said Adam.

That feeling of dread again. Where was Mum? No good looking now in the dark, but first thing in the morning...

'If you let us stay here tonight,' I

said, ‘you can come with us tomorrow to get food from our car.’

‘OK, but only because I’ve hardly any food left. You can sleep in the other bedroom.’

I pulled the packet of biscuits out of my pocket.

‘Here. Have a couple of these. I’m Grace. This is Adam and Ruby.’

‘Dave,’ he said, and led the way up the rickety stairs.

Chapter Four

We huddled together on the damp mattress. I'd never been so cold. What if Ruby and Adam died from hypothermia? I was supposed to look after them.

Scrabbling sounds. Downstairs I'd seen dead mice and dead rats. What if there were live ones? I'd wedged a broken chair against the door, but it wasn't that secure.

When I woke it was light. I was stiff, shivering, squashed against the wall, Ruby's sharp knees sticking into my back. Adam snored on the other side of her. The chair was still wedged against the door.

My mouth tasted foul.

'Let's get back to the car,' I said, 'and get our stuff.'

Dave was already downstairs.

'Come on,' I said. 'Food! We'll feel loads better after a hot meal.'

He smirked, but I ignored him.

He walked behind us. That suited me. He must have been wearing the same clothes for ages. He really stank.

In the fields there were huge pools of water and mounds of earth. The wind blew that dreadful smell into our faces. Those mounds - they weren't earth. They were dead cattle and sheep.

We passed the petrol-station.

Why was everywhere so quiet? The ordinary country sounds of birds

and animals and tractors were missing.

'We should be able to see the roundabout,' said Adam.

'There isn't one,' said Dave.

The wide road stretched ahead, absolutely straight, for a mile or more. The roundabout had disappeared, and so had the road that should have led us back to the car.

Where was it? Where was Mum? And where on earth were we?

Chapter Five

'You liar!' Dave spat the words into my face. 'There's no car, and no food!'

'I don't tell lies.'

'We definitely came this way last

night,' said Adam, 'from the car, to the roundabout and past the filling-station to the cottage.'

'We must find Mr Mason,' I said.

'I told you, he doesn't exist,' said Dave, and he walked off back the way we'd come.

'Let him go,' I said. 'We're better off without him. Let's find Mr Mason.'

At the bottom of the hill, instead of Mr Mason's house, there was a large modern bungalow, next to a flooded field, with twenty or more caravans, smashed and ripped apart, several

completely flattened like empty cardboard boxes. And there was a sign: GREENFIELDS CARAVAN SITE.

'It's weird,' I said. 'Some things are the same, but some are totally different.'

'Parallel worlds,' said Adam.

'What?' asked Ruby.

'Worlds existing at the same time, side by side, like parallel lines, so they don't usually meet,' said Adam. 'Miss Hardy told us about them in science.'

'That sounds stupid,' said Ruby.

At that moment Dave appeared

from round the corner of a tumbled-down barn.

'See!' He waved his arm towards the caravans. 'The floods *did* happen.'

'Prove it!' I said.

'OK. Come down to the village, and I'll show you.'

Chapter Six

It was different from how I remembered. Instead of old cottages with flowery gardens there were modern houses, with long, paved driveways and huge patios. Where the playing-field had been was an enormous car park full of smashed-up cars, heaps of tangled metal, and a building – must have been a supermarket – with the front torn away, as if a tidal wave had swept through.

The stench made me want to throw up. Rubbish everywhere: plastic bags, bottles, dead animals, mounds of clothes and shoes...

Then I realised...

I pulled Ruby away.

'Isn't there somewhere we can have something to eat and get warm?' asked Adam.

'There isn't any food,' said Dave.

'The rats ate it. There's no water, electricity, gas, or oil.'

'We'll collect wood and make a fire,' I said.

'It's soaking wet, stupid! You can't light it.'

'Are we going to die?' asked Ruby.

'Of course not,' I snapped. 'But we've got to help ourselves. It's no good just trailing round the streets.'

'Got a better idea then?' asked Dave.

'If we climb the church tower we'll be able to see for miles,' I said. 'We might see smoke from chimneys, other people–'

'There's no point,' said Dave.

'We're going,' I said. 'It's up to you whether you come or not.'

The floodwater must have swept into the church with tremendous force. The solid wooden door had been lifted off its hinges, smashed on to the stone floor. There were piles of broken wood.

'Those were the pews.'

Dave had followed us. He looked very sad, standing alone amid the wreckage.

'I'm glad you came,' I said. 'We must stick together.'

The little door at the bottom of the tower was gone, swept away by the water surging up the spiral stone staircase.

At the top we stepped out on to the roof.

Chapter Seven

The lighthouse had gone; cliffs had crumbled, houses had fallen into the sea. One huge sheet of water surrounded us. I couldn't tell where land ended or sea began. Sticking up out of the water were broken masts, splintered fencing, smashed wind-turbines, houses with gaping holes in roofs and walls.

'I'm sorry, Dave,' I said. 'You were right.'

'I wish I wasn't. It was all on satellite-vision. Floods all over the world – typhoons, tsunamis. Then here. It never stopped raining; rivers burst their banks, dams collapsed, electricity and power stations were flooded. Millions of tons of water, and nowhere for it to go.'

'Why?' asked Ruby.

'Because we've built all over the

flood-plains. We've paved and concreted gardens, torn down hedges, cut down forests. We've driven everywhere, flown all over the world, built more and more power stations–'

'Are you talking about climate change?' I asked.

'Yeah. It makes me so angry. It's our fault.' He paused. 'There was this emergency broadcast. The Thames Barrier was closed, but a wall of water, a hundred feet high, swept through it. Then the screen went blank–'

He folded his arms tightly across

his chest. I touched his shoulder.

'What happened here?'

'A tidal wave came down the east coast from Scotland. Gale-force winds. High tide. The sea-level was over four metres. It went right over the sea-defences. Cliffs collapsed. Rivers, the Broads, all overflowed. Nobody could escape.'

'Except you,' said Ruby.

'Yeah, the noise of the storm woke me. I ran outside to look for Mum and Dad. Our river burst its bank. They were trying to save the cattle, but the flood-water swept them both away-'

'We're like orphans too,' said Ruby. She squeezed his hand.

Dave was completely alone. At least we had each other, even in this world.

Then Ruby piped up, 'I'm hungry.'

'Plenty of dead animals,' said Adam.

'Eeurgh!'

'Bad idea,' said Dave. 'They've been rotting away for weeks. What with that and the pesticides in the soil, everything's contaminated.'

'We can't stay in *this* world,' I said. 'We've got to get back to ours.

Go back to the roundabout. That's where we left our world and walked into this one.'

'Are you sure that's where it was?' asked Adam.

'Well, I *think* that's where the road first seemed different, and where the fog suddenly lifted.'

'But the roundabout's not there,' said Adam.

'Then we've got to work out where it would be in our world. Ruby, how long did it take us last night to walk from the roundabout to the cottage?'

'Can't remember,' she said. 'I can't think straight. I'm hungry.'

'Why don't we go back to the cottage,' said Dave. 'There's a bit of food left – not much, but we'll feel better if we have something to eat.'

Chapter Eight

On the kitchen table – eight small potatoes.

'Eeurgh!' said Ruby. 'I can't eat raw potato.'

I rubbed the soil off and peeled

them, cutting them into little chunks.

'Pretend it's something you really like,' said Dave, 'like pineapple.'

Ruby pulled a face but managed a few tiny pieces.

'Now, Ruby,' I said. 'Close your eyes and imagine you're back at the roundabout, looking at the watch.'

'Twenty past – I think.'

Then I remembered. When we got to the cottage I'd pushed Ruby's coat-sleeve back, and looked at my watch, hanging loosely on her skinny wrist. I could see it in my mind's eye.

'It was quarter to seven when we got here,' I said.

'So it took twenty-five minutes from the roundabout,' said Adam. 'What time is it now, Ruby?'

'Five minutes past eleven.'

'Let's set off now and time ourselves,' said Adam. 'We can walk at a steady pace towards the roundabout and then stop at half-past.'

I wasn't sure this would work, but I couldn't think of anything else.

It was a dead-straight road with flooded fields on either side. It all looked the same. We were trapped in this awful sameness. Could we find a way out?

'I don't know what I'm looking for,' I said.

'What about something that looks really out of place?' said Dave.

'That makes sense, even though your world and ours aren't very different apart from the flooding.'

I was trying to work out how far ahead the roundabout should be. Would we recognise the way back to our own world? I so longed to be there. What if we never found it? We'd no food, no clean drinking-water. I knew people could survive a long time without food, but not without water, and if we drank contaminated water we'd get terrible diseases.

'It's half-past,' said Ruby.

But we hadn't seen anything that

reminded us of our world.

Then I heard something – a bird singing. There it was! – a smudge of orangey-red against the wet brown earth.

'Look – a robin.'

'What?' asked Dave.

'A robin,' said Ruby, 'a bird. Don't you have them?'

'No.'

'That could mean our world's very close,' said Adam. 'It must have found its way here, slipped through a tiny gap. But we're a lot bigger.'

'Still we did get through the gap into this world last night,' I said. 'I think we took the wrong exit – turned off the roundabout before we should, and ended up here.'

'Perhaps our two worlds sort of collided in the fog,' said Ruby.

'Something like that,' said Adam.

'If we're kind and feed the robin perhaps it'll show us the way back,' said Ruby.

I felt in my pockets – something gritty under my fingernails. Biscuit crumbs!

Chapter Nine

I scooped out some crumbs for each of us, but Dave shook his head.

'I can't leave here until I'm certain there's nobody left. I'll walk inland, as far as Northwic. There might be survivors there. I couldn't settle in your world, thinking I might have left someone behind.'

'But how will you follow us?' asked Ruby.

'After you've gone I'll build a cairn on the roadside here with those flints to mark the spot, and hope the robin

comes back,' said Dave.

I found a pen, folded a clean tissue, and printed our address and phone number. I gave it to Dave.

'If you follow us get in touch.'

'Yeah.'

The robin still sang its thin, sweet song, but it could fly away any minute.

'Let's feed it now,' I said.

Adam held out his hand. The robin stopped singing, shifted position slightly. Was it getting ready to take off? Then it put its head on one side, hopped on to Adam's wrist and pecked away until all the crumbs had gone.

Adam's edges went fuzzy, as if he was squeezing sideways through a very narrow slit. And he was gone.

He was holding Ruby's hand, pulling her after him. She held out the crumbs in her other hand to the robin. Her outline went wavy, and she grabbed my hand. I held out my crumbs. What if the robin wouldn't come to me?

His sharp little beak pecked at the palm of my hand. I had a last glimpse of Dave, standing alone; then my eyes closed of their own accord...

Chapter Ten

In front – the roundabout. Behind – the road to Little Thornton; narrow and winding, a country lane bordered by trees and hedges. A robin sang.

In the distance – the petrol-station.

'We'd better ask if Mum was there last night,' I said.

I grabbed Ruby's hand, and then Adam's. If he didn't like his big sister holding his hand, too bad! But he squeezed my hand tightly and grinned at me.

We were definitely back in our own world. Cars drove in and out of the petrol-station. It was such a relief.

'Let's get something to eat,' said Ruby.

'Good idea!' said Adam.

We walked across the forecourt to the shop. There were racks of newspapers outside. The headlines were a bit of a shock:

EASTERN GAZETTE
Monday, 22 December 2008
MISSING CHILDREN

Below was a photo of Mum, Adam, Ruby and me.

'Look at us!' said Ruby.

We were home again with Mum in just a few hours.

She was hugging us, and telling us off, and laughing and crying, all at the same time.

Of course, she didn't believe us when we said we'd been in another world.

'You got lost in the fog,' she said. 'You must have been wandering about all night in the freezing cold. No wonder you're imagining things!'

But we know different.

Dave hasn't appeared yet, but we haven't given up hope. If he does turn up one day, Mum will have to believe us.